This book belongs to

Murphy Hansen   5/2012

For all our great-nephews and nieces
T.B.~B. & J.B.~B.

Text copyright © Tiziana Bendall-Brunello 2010
Illustrations copyright © John Bendall-Brunello 2010

This edition published by Parragon in 2010

Parragon
Queen Street House
4 Queen Street
Bath BA1 1HE, UK

Published by arrangement with Meadowside Children's Books
185 Fleet Street London EC4A 2HS

ISBN 978-1-4454-3689-0

Printed in China

My Favorite Food

Tiziana & John Bendall-Brunello

Bath · New York · Singapore · Hong Kong · Cologne · Delhi
Melbourne · Amsterdam · Johannesburg · Auckland · Shenzhen

Little Goose and her mommy were in the yard, enjoying some fresh, green grass.

"Mmm . . . I love grass," said Little Goose. "It's my favorite food!

I wonder if everybody
loves grass as much as me?"

"Why don't you go and
find out," said Mommy.

So off went little Goose to
find out Pig's favorite food . . .

"What's your favorite food, Pig?"
she asked.

"Apples,"

said Pig. "They're so juicy!"

"Mmm," said Little Goose, "I like apples too.
I wonder what Goat's favorite food is?"

So off she went to find out . . .

"What's your favorite food, Goat?"
asked Little Goose.

"Socks,"
said Goat. "They're so chewy!"

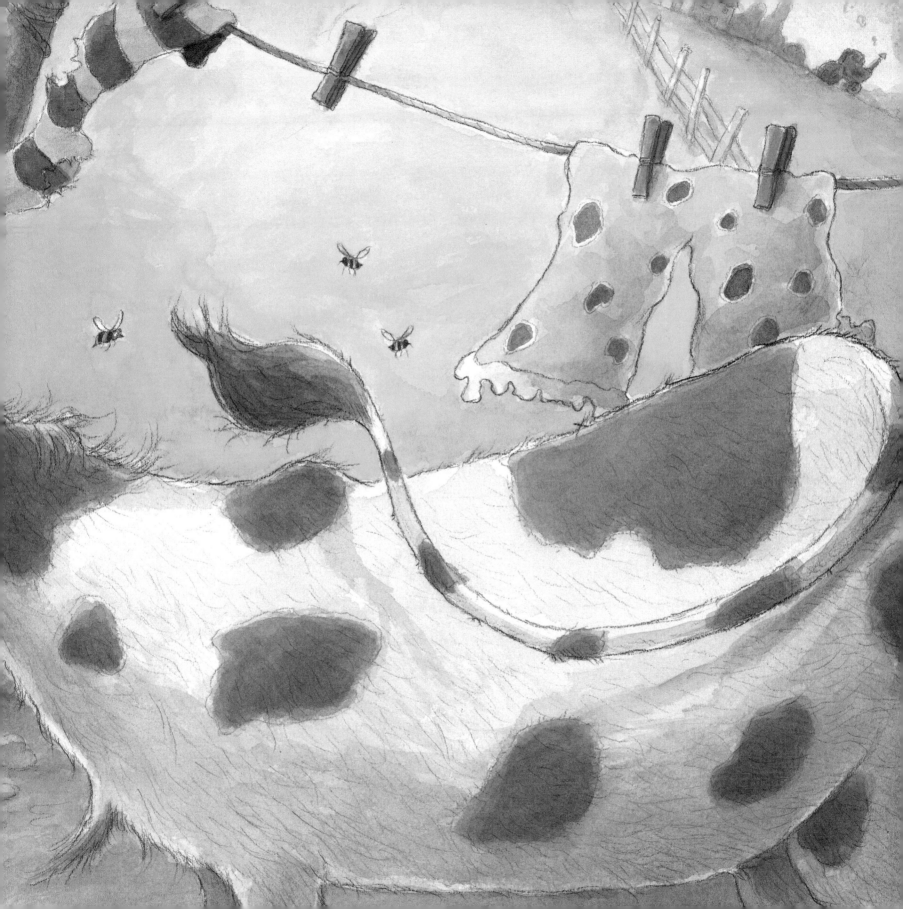

"Hmmm," said Little Goose,
"I'm not sure I like socks!

I wonder what Cow's favorite food is?"

So off she went to find out . . .

"What's your favorite food, Cow?" asked Little Goose.

"Daisies," said Cow. "They're so sweet!"

"Mmm," said Little Goose, "daisies are tasty.
But I wonder what Fox's
favorite food is?"

So off she went to find out . . .

"Fox! Fox! What's your favorite food?" asked Little Goose.

"Well . . ." said Fox,
"let me think.
My favorite food is . . ."

"YOU!"

"Yikes!" squealed Little Goose.
And she ran away as fast as her
little legs would carry her . . .

... safely back into
the loving wings
of her mommy.

And while Little Goose enjoyed some of her
favorite food—grass—

Fox settled down to eat his favorite food—strawberries!